Basketball's Greatest Players

Bob Italia

Published by Abdo & Daughters, 4940 Viking Drive, Suite 622, Edina, Minnesota 55435.

Library bound edition distributed by Rockbottom Books, Pentagon Tower, P.O. Box 36036, Minneapolis, Minnesota 55435. International copyrights reserved in all countries. No part of this book may be reproduced in any form without written permission from the publisher. Printed in the United States.

Cover Photo By: Allsport, Inc.
Interior Photos by: Allsport, Inc.

Edited By: Rosemary Wallner

Library of Congress Cataloging-in-Publication Data

Italia, Robert, 1955-
    Basketball's Greatest Players/by Bob Italia.
        p.   cm. -- (The Year in Sports)
    Includes Glossary.
    ISBN 1-56239-243-3
    1. Basketball players -- United States -- Rating of -- Juvenile Literature. I. Title.
II. Series: Year in Sports (Edina, Minn.).
    GV884.A1I85 1993
    796.323'092'2--dc20   93-11976
    [B]   CIP
                                        AC

Contents

How Basketball Awards Are Determined

In any sport, players strive to do their best each season. After the season ends, sportswriters, league players, and coaches look at statistics and compare performances. That's when the fans find out who was the best of the best.

In the National Basketball (NBA), a 96-member panel of local and national pro basketball writers and broadcasters votes for most of the major awards. The NBA head coaches vote for the All-Rookie team and the All-Defensive team.

Most Valuable Player

The Maurice Podoloff Trophy is awarded to the player judged to be the most valuable to his team. The award is named after Maurice Podoloff, the first commissioner of the NBA. From 1956-1980, winners were selected by the NBA players. Afterwards, a national panel of professional basketball writers and broadcasters voted for the winners. Players who have high scoring averages usually win this award.

A list of past winners attests to this fact: Michael Jordan (1992, 30.1-point average), Larry Bird (1985, 28.7-point average), Moses Malone (1982, 31.1-point average), Kareem Abdul-Jabbar (1972, 34.8-point average), and Wilt Chamberlain (1966, 33.5-point average).

Michael Jordan's ability to score helped make him an MVP.

On rare occasions, a dominant defensive player will win the award: center Wes Unseld (1969, 13.8-point average) and center Bill Russell (1965, 14.1-point average) are good examples. They intimidated other teams with their physical strength and presence, and controlled the backboards with their rebounding power.

Multiple winners include Kareem Abdul-Jabbar (6), Bill Russell (5), Wilt Chamberlain (4), Larry Bird, Magic Johnson, Michael Jordan, and Moses Malone (3), and Bob Pettit (2), who was the first league MVP in 1956.

Larry Bird's versatility on the court helped to make him an MVP.

The 1993 Most Valuable Player

When he played for the Philadelphia 76ers, center Charles Barkley was a star player on an average team. Then after the 1992 season, Barkley left the 76ers and headed west to the Phoenix Suns. Phoenix was a good team—but could Barkley make them great? The critics wondered.

Barkley wasted no time to prove that he was the kind of player that could lift an entire team to greatness. Phoenix bolted to the early divisional lead—and never looked back. They won their division and racked up the best record for the 1992-93 NBA season (62-20).

"Sir Charles" averaged 25.6 points per game and 12.2 rebounds. Even more remarkable, he dished off a career-high 5.1 assists per game. Though the Suns eventually fell to the Chicago Bulls in the NBA finals, Barley proved   the he and the Suns were among the NBA's best. No doubt he   and the Suns will be back in the playoffs next year.

"When you talk about the top forces in the game of basketball," said Houston Rockets guard Kenny Smith, "Charles is among the group. He can hurt you in so many ways."

"Chuck is largely responsible for the success we've had," admitted Suns head coach Paul Westphal. "He's gotten a tremendous amount of help from his teammates, but his attitude and toughness have been the key to our record and success."

Most Valuable Player

Year		Pos.	Pts.
1993	Charles Barkley	C	25.6
1992	Michael Jordan	G	30.1
1991	Michael Jordan	G	31.5
1990	Magic Johnson	G	22.3
1989	Magic Johnson	G	22.5

Rookie of the Year

The Eddie Gottlieb Trophy is awarded to the outstanding rookie of the regular season. It is named after the pro basketball pioneer and owner-coach of the first NBA champion, the Philadelphia Warriors. Winners are selected by a 96-member national panel of pro basketball writers and broadcasters. The first award went to Don Meineke of Fort Wayne Pistons (1953). He had a 10.8-point scoring average.

Many outstanding rookies become outstanding veteran players. Michael Jordan (1985), Larry Bird (1980), Lew Alcindor (1970), Willis Reed (1965), and Oscar Robertson (1961) were all winning rookies. They became some of the greatest players of all time.

Winning Rookie of the Year honors does not guarantee a successful career, however. What ever happened to rookie winners Ralph Sampson (1984) Ernie DiGregorio (1974), or Geoff Petrie (1971)?

And just because a player isn't named Rookie of the Year does not mean he will be unsuccessful. Scottie Pippen, Dominique Wilkins, Karl Malone, Charles Barkley, and Hakeem Olajuwon (just to name a few) did not receive the award. Yet they became well known and respected players.

The 1993 Rookie of the Year

Few players—not even Michael Jordan—arrive in the NBA with as much attention as the 1993 winner, Shaquille O'Neal. The Orlando Magic center has already been compared with Hall-of-Fame members Wilt Chamberlain and Bill Russell. Because of O'Neal's rare combination of size, strength, and quickness, some think he might be even better. Time will tell.

For now, the seven-foot one-inch, 300-pound O'Neal has cleared one important hurdle. He helped carry his team to within a game of the playoffs while standing toe-to-toe with some of the game's best big men. Not only was he the best rookie, he established himself as one of the league's top stars.

Shaquille O'Neal has the skills to become the best center in NBA history.

Rookie of the Year

Year	Pos.	Pts.
1993 Shaquille O'Neal	C	23.4
1992 Larry Johnson	F	19.2
1991 Derrick Coleman	F	18.4
1990 David Robinson	C	24.3
1989 Mitch Richmond	G	22.0
1988 Mark Jackson	G	13.6

O'Neal averaged 23.4 points per game, 13.9 rebounds, and 3.53 blocked shots per game. His statistics were similar to those of league MVP Charles Barkley.

Even more, O'Neal's arrival in the NBA had a direct impact on attendance around the league. Wherever O'Neal played, basketball arenas became sold out. Everyone around the country wanted to see this amazing and dominant rookie talent.

"The guy's an impressive basketball player," said New York Knicks Coach Pat Riley. "He's very young, and he's going to get nothing but better and better."

Watch out, Michael Jordan. Here comes the "Shaq."

Defensive Player of the Year

Without a doubt, the offense gets most of the attention in the newspapers, sports magazines, and television news shows. After all, what can be more exciting than a slam dunk by Michael Jordan or a three-pointer by Dan Majerle? How about Horace Grant blocking Kevin Johnson's jump shot in Game 6 to win the NBA finals?

The offense may get the most attention, but if your team can't play defense, you won't win in the NBA. The New York Knicks, Chicago Bulls, Houston Rockets, and the Cleveland Cavaliers were the top four defensive teams in the league. They were also among the best teams in the league.

Because defense is just as important as offense, the Defensive Player of the Year award was created in 1983 to honor the best defensive player for the regular season. The winners are often big men—centers or power forwards who can block shots, clog the lane, intimidate offensive players, and haul down rebound after rebound. Past winners include David Robinson (1992), Dennis Rodman (1990-91), and Mark Eaton (1985 & 1989).

Michael Jordan, the 1988 Defensive Player of the Year.

Occasionally, quick and agile guards win the award. They can intercept passes or strip the ball from opposing players. Players like Michael Jordan (1988), Alvin Robertson (1986), and Sidney Moncrief fit that mold.

Winners are selected by a national panel of professional basketball writers and broadcasters. The first winner was guard Sidney Moncrief of the Milwaukee Bucks. Multiple winners include Mark Eaton, Sidney Moncrief, Dennis Rodman, and Michael Jordan.

The 1993 Defensive Player of the Year

The 1993 Defensive Player of the Year was center Hakeem Olajuwon of the Houston Rockets. Most people think of Olajuwon as a scoring machine (which he is). Olajuwon led the Rockets with 2,140 total points, field goals made (848), and free throws made (444).

But what make him so dangerous on the court is his ability to anticipate plays, force turnovers, steal the ball, and block shots. His defensive ability has often turned the momentum of a game around in his team's favor. When you consider that Olajuwon is a center, his defensive statistics are even more amazing. Olajuwon led the Rockets in most defensive categories, including blocked shots (342), steals (150), and rebounds (1,068).

Hakeem Olajuwon was the NBA's best defensive player in 1993.

Defensive Player of the Year

Year		Pos.
1993	Hakeem Olajuwon	C
1992	David Robinson	C
1991	Dennis Rodman	F
1990	Dennis Rodman	F
1989	Mark Eaton	C
1988	Michael Jordan	G

The Sixth Man Award

Basketball is a grueling sport. Not only does it take much physical stamina to run up and down the court the entire game, it also take a lot of physical strength. Basketball is a lot rougher than it seems. While most spectators watch the ball, the players battle each other for position. All this pounding can take a lot out of the starting players. That's why teams need extra players who can come off the bench without warming up and immediately contribute.

Some bench players are better than others. They can come in and maintain the lead that the starting team has established while the star players get a much needed rest. All good teams have a "sixth man" who helps the team win important games. The Bulls have John Paxson. The Knicks have Doc Rivers. And the Portland Trail Blazers have this year's Sixth Man Award winner, Cliff Robinson.

The Sixth Man Award was created in 1983 to honor the best off-the-bench player for the regular season. Winners are selected by a national panel of pro basketball writers and broadcasters. The first winner was Bobby Jones of the Philadelphia 76ers. Multiple winners include Kevin McHale, Ricky Pierce, and Detlef Schrempf.

Detlef Schrempf won the Sixth Man award in 1991 & 1992.

15

The 1993 Sixth Man Award Winner

Cliff Robinson proved to be an invaluable player for the Portland Trail Blazers. Coming off the bench, Robinson averaged a career-high 19,1 points and continued his strong defense.

Amazingly, Robinson led the Blazers in total points scored (1,570), field goals made (632), and blocked shots (163). He also tied for the most points scored in one game (40)—not bad for someone who often came off the bench during each game.

The Sixth Man Award

Year		Pos.
1993	Cliff Robinson	F
1992	Detlef Schrempf	F
1991	Detlef Schrempf	F
1990	Ricky Pierce	G
1989	Eddie Johnson	F
1988	Roy Tarpley	C

Coach of the Year

Sometimes the coach of a basketball team can make the difference between winning and losing. Coaches call the plays, set the defenses, and choose the starting lineup. They must also deal with multimillion dollar egos and get everyone to play as a team.

The Red Auerbach Trophy honors those outstanding coaches who make a difference. The award was renamed in 1967 for the former Boston coach who led the Celtics to nine NBA titles. Winners are selected by a national panel of pro basketball writers and broadcasters.

Multiple winners include Don Nelson (3), Bill Fitch, Cotton Fitzsimmons, and Gene Shue (2). The first winner was Harry Gallatin of the St. Louis Hawks (1963).

Cotton Fitzsimmons won the Coach of the Year award in 1989 while with the Phoenix Suns.

The 1993 Coach of the Year

In 1993, no coach did more for his club than New York Knicks coach Pat Riley. A former Los Angeles Laker coach, Riley guided the Knicks to one of their best seasons ever.

The Knicks won 60 regular-season games—including a 37-4 record at home—to win the Atlantic Division and earn home-court advantage throughout the playoffs. In two seasons with the Knicks, Riley has compiled an impressive 111-53 record.

The playoff loss to the Chicago Bulls in the Eastern Conference Finals was a huge disappointment. But with Riley guiding the team, the Knicks have become favorites to finally capture the NBA crown.

Coach of the Year

Year	Coach
1993	Pat Riley (New York Knicks)
1992	Don Nelson (Golden State Warriors)
1991	Don Chaney (Houston Rockets)
1990	Pat Riley (Los Angeles Lakers)
1989	Cotton Fitzsimmons (Phoenix Suns)
1988	Doug Moe (Denver Nuggets)

Pat Riley—the 1993 NBA Coach of the Year.

GUARD

JOHN STOCKTON

CENTER

HAKEEM
OLAJUWON

FORWARD

KARL MALONE

The NBA All-Star Team

Pos.	Player	Team	Pts.	Rebs.	Pct.
G	Michael Jordan	Bulls	32.6	6.6	49.5
G	John Stockton	Jazz	15.1	2.8	48.6
F	Karl Malone	Jazz	27.0	11.2	55.2
F	Charles Barkley	Suns	25.6	12.2	52.0
C	Hakeem Olajuwon	Rockets	26.1	13.0	52.9

FORWARD

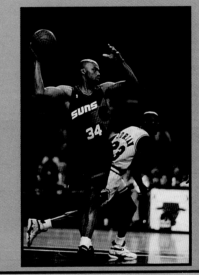

CHARLES BARKLEY

GUARD

MICHAEL JORDAN

Offensive Leaders

Team Offense

In 1993, no team scored more points or more often than the Phoenix Suns. Led by league MVP Charles Barkley, the Suns averaged 113.4 points per game with 9289 total points scored. The Charlotte Hornets were a distant second with a 110.1 average with 9030 total points scored.

In addition to Barkley's 25.6 points per game, the Suns were led by Dan Majerle (16.9), Kevin Johnson (16.1), Richard Dumas (15.8), Cedric Ceballos (12.8), Tom Chambers (12.2), and Danny Ainge (11.8). Phoenix was held below 100 points only 9 games (the league's best). The Suns defeated their opponents by 10 points or more a league-high 34 times.

Dan Majerle (above) and Kevin Johnson (opposite page) transformed the Phoenix Suns into a scoring machine.

Michael Jordan won his seventh straight scoring championship in 1993.

Leading Scorer

No surprises here. For the seventh year in a row, Michael Jordan led the league in scoring with a 32.6 points-per-game average. Jordan also scored the most points in one game—64 against the Orlando Magic on January 16. In that same game, Jordan had the most field goal attempts in one game (49) and the most field goals made (27).

In addition to his field goals, Jordan sunk a team-best 81 three-pointers and made 476 free throws. His 2,541 total points were also a league-best.

Assist Leader

Playmaking can be just as important as scoring. Without someone who consistently passes to the open man on a given play, a team cannot hope to win.

For the sixth year in a row, the 1993 assist leader was guard John Stockton of the Utah Jazz. Stockton is considered the top passing guard in the NBA. His ability to push the ball up the court and thread the needle while at full gallop is unrivaled. Stockton knows what passes to make even when the fast break opportunities are not there. He also knows when to pull back and run a slower, half-court game.

For the season, the 6-foot one-inch, 175-pound Stockton had 987 total assists for a 12.0 average. Tim Hardaway of the Golden State Warriors was second with 699 total assists for a 10.6 average.

"Stockton has great vision of the floor and really knows where all his guys are," said Lenny Wilkens. "He knows precisely when and where to deliver the ball to the right guy. He has a great feel for the game, like all great point guards."

John Stockton of the Utah Jazz is one of the NBA's top playmakers. Left unguarded, he can become a scoring threat as well.

Field Goal Percentage

Sharpshooters can be a tremendous asset to a team. When a basket must be made, a play can be designed to get the ball into the hands of a player most likely to sink the field goal. A player who makes half of his field goals is considered good. (Leading scorer Michael Jordan had a .495 field goal percentage.) The top players in this category sink more baskets than they miss.

In 1993, Cedric Ceballos of the Phoenix Suns was the deadliest offensive player. He made 381 of 662 field goal attempts for a league-high .576 field goal percentage. Brad Daugherty of the Cleveland Cavaliers was second with a .571 percentage.

Cedric Ceballos of the Phoenix Suns slam-dunked his way to the NBA's best shooting percentage.

Free Throw Percentage

Most games are won or lost on the freethrow line. That's why it's important for any team to work hard on their free throw accuracy. Some players have a special talent for sinking free throws. They sink 75-80 percent of their free throw attempts. But the leading free throw specialists elevate the task to greater heights, as the following list will attest.

The top free throw shooter in 1993 was Mark Price of the Cleveland Cavaliers. Price sank 289 of 305 free throw attempts for a .948 percentage. Chris Jackson of the Denver Nuggets was second with a .935 percentage.

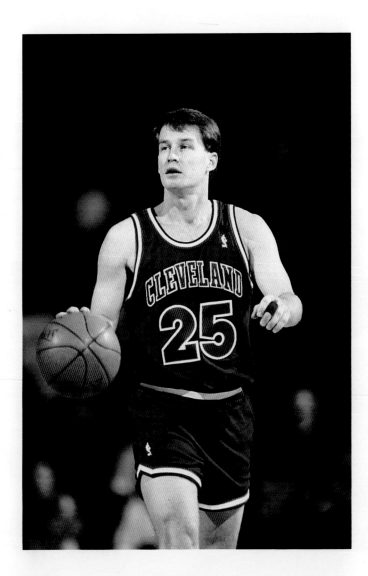

Mark Price of the Cleveland Cavaliers was the NBA's best freethrow shooter.

Defensive Leaders

Team Defense

In 1993, no team threw up a greater wall of defense than the New York Knicks. Led by Patrick Ewing, Charles Oakley, and Anthony Mason, the Knicks defense swarmed and smothered the opponents offense. New York allowed a league-low 7,823 total points for a league-best 95.4 average. The Chicago Bulls were second with a 98.9 average.

In a game against Chicago on November 28, the Knicks allowed the Bulls only 28 field goals. On February 14, the Knicks hauled down a league-best 73 rebounds against the Orlando Magic.

Charles Oakley (left) and Patrick Ewing (opposite page) anchored a rock-solid defense for the New York Knicks.

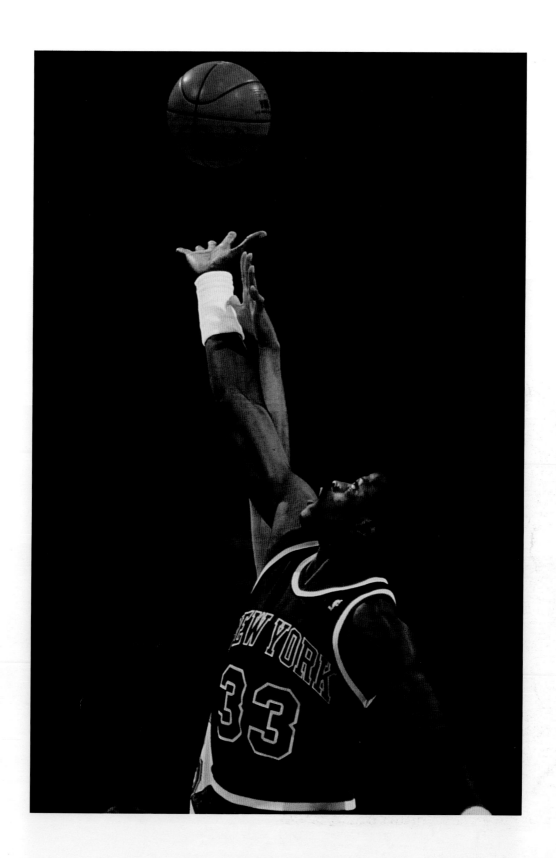

Rebounding

You would think that the NBA's top rebounder would have to be one of its most powerful players—Patrick Ewing, Shaquille O'Neal, or maybe David Robinson. Not so. For the second year in a row, the leading rebounder was Dennis Rodman of the Detroit Pistons—and it wasn't even close. Rodman snatched 1, 132 rebounds for a 18.3 average. Shaquille O'Neal was a distant second with a 13.9 average.

The 6-foot eight-inch, 210-pound Rodman is considered a small forward. Many of his rebounds come from hard work and determination. "There may be 100 guys in the NBA who have the talent to do what Dennis did," said former coach Chuck Daly. "But they don't have that special desire. Rodman is one of a kind."

Blocked Shots

The top shot blocker for 1993 was Houston center Hakeem Olajuwon. The 6-foot ten-inch, 250-pound Olajuwon used his great athleticism and jumping ability to lead the league with 342 blocked shots and a 4.17 average. Shaquille O'Neal was a distant second with 286 blocked shots and a 3.53 average.

Key to Abbreviations

Ast	Assists
Avg.	Average
Blk	Blocked Shots
C	Center
F	Forward
Fg	Field Goals
Fga	Field Goals Attempted
Fg%	Field Goal Percentage
Ft	Free Throws
Fta	Free Throws Attempted
Ft%	Free Throw Percentage
G	Games/Guard
L	Losses
MP	Minutes Played
Orb	Offensive Rebounds
Pf	Personal Fouls
Ppg	Points Per Game
Pts.	Points
Reb	Rebounds
Stl	Steals
To	Turnovers
W	Wins

Glossary

Assist—A pass of the ball to the teammate scoring a goal.

Center—A player who holds the middle position on the court.

Forward—A player who is part of the front line of offense and defense.

Free Throw—A Privilege given a player to score one point by an unhindered throw for goal from within the freethrow circle and behind the freethrow line.

Guard—Either of two players who initiate plays from the center of the court.

Jump Ball—To put the ball in play in the center restraining circle with a jump between two opponents at the beginning of the game and each extra period.

Personal Foul—A player foul which involves contact with an opponent while the ball is alive or after the ball is in possession of a player for a throw-in.